STEVIE
The Rebel

Home Farm Twins

Stevie
The Rebel

Jenny Oldfield

Illustrated by Kate Aldous

*Hodder
Children's
Books*

a division of Hodder Headline plc

First published in Great Britain in 1997
by Hodder Children's Books
a division of Hodder Headline plc
338 Euston Road
London NW1 3BH

10 9 8 7 6 5 4 3 2 1

A Catalogue record for this book is available from the British Library

ISBN 0 340 68992 7

Typeset by Avon Dataset Ltd, Bidford-on-Avon, Warks

Printed and bound in Great Britain by
Cox & Wyman Ltd, Reading, Berks

One

'That pig is eating us out of house and home!' David Moore grumbled.

Helen and Hannah's pet pig, Sunny, chomped his way through a trough full of vegetables. He was round, pink, smooth and fat. His curly tail wiggled as he ate.

The twins sat on the farmyard wall at Home Farm. Speckle, their Border collie, lay stretched out along the wall top beside them. It was a perfect Spring day; Doveton Lake sparkled in the valley below, and the sun shone in a sky the colour of a blackbird's egg.

'Give me a horse to feed any day!' Their dad shook his head as the pig gobbled down the last shred of cabbage. 'A nice, good-natured pony like Solo would do me, full stop!'

Solo, the twins' grey pony, snickered. He knew when he was being praised.

Hannah patted the pig's neck. 'Sunny's only doing what all pigs do,' she protested.

'Yes, getting fat at my expense!' He turned out his empty pockets and frowned.

'You'll see,' Helen promised. 'When Sunny's a champion pig winning loads of prizes, you'll be glad we've got him.'

David Moore scratched his head. 'If Sunny starts winning rosettes at the shows, I'll eat my words,' he agreed. 'If the pig doesn't eat them first!'

The twins giggled. Helen jumped down from the wall and went to give Sunny a bruised apple which she'd kept hidden in her pocket. She scratched his sturdy sides with a stick and watched him chomp at the fruit. Meanwhile, Solo came up and nuzzled at her pocket. 'How did you know I had one for you too?' she murmured, as she took out a second apple and gave it to him.

'Who wants to come to Dorothy Miller's place with me to take pictures of her donkeys?' David Moore said casually. Then he stood back to avoid the rush.

'Me!' Hannah leaped from the wall.

Speckle barked and bounded after her.

'Wait for me!' Helen almost tripped as she ran headlong for the wall and scrambled over it. Solo and Sunny stood in the field looking put out by her sudden departure. 'Sorry!' She glanced back at them before she jumped down to join Hannah and her dad in the farmyard. 'We're going to see a donkey sanctuary; we won't be long!'

Their dad told them that he had promised to take some photographs for posters advertising the Open Day at Lake View. The pictures would show cute donkeys in need of good homes. People would see the posters and fall in love with the homeless donkeys. Then they would come along next weekend and offer to help Dorothy look after her charges. At least that was what was meant to happen. The twins' dad had promised to do the photos for nothing.

'I wonder if there's such a thing as a *pig* sanctuary?' he said as they got into the car and drove off down the lane.

'Da-ad!' Hannah and Helen said in the same breath.

'How could you?'

'Don't even think about it!'

They swept down the hill into Doveton village, past the Saunders' posh manor house, along the main street.

'But listen, these sanctuaries are nice places, most of them. Sunny would be well looked after. Plenty of other pigs to talk to, nice warm pigsty, *lots* of food!' He waved at Luke Martin who stood in his shop doorway. 'Wait until we get to Dorothy's donkey place; you'll see what I mean.'

'Never!' Hannah said.

'Over my dead body!' Helen played along.

Their dad always grumbled about the cost of keeping their animals fed and watered. But just this morning, they'd crept up and found him on his hands and knees in the field, actually talking to Sunny! Really, he was as mad about animals as they were.

'Lake View is a luxury hotel for donkeys,' he promised as they pulled out of the valley and up the far side of the fell. 'Come on, I'll show you what I mean!'

The donkey sanctuary stood in a sheltered corner of the mountainside, just off the winding main road which led to Nesfield. Lake View was big and white, with gables and outbuildings, surrounded by a neat garden with roses, fruit trees and lawns. But Helen and Hannah hardly noticed the house.

There was a field in front where Dorothy Miller kept her donkeys; dozens of them, of all shapes and sizes. Black donkeys, rusty donkeys, dull brown donkeys. White ones and chestnuts, dappled and piebald. There were donkeys with striped legs, donkeys with stiff, spiky manes or floppy ones that fell into their eyes. Creaky old donkeys glanced up at the sound of the Moores' car, then grazed on. Young stallions and fillies came trotting to peek over the wall as they passed by. And two tiny grey foals tottered to their feet to come and look.

'Oh, Dad, stop!' Hannah breathed. The little twins came wobbling towards the wall.

He drew up at the bottom of the drive.

Helen and Hannah leaped out, telling Speckle to stay in the car. And now all the donkeys came galloping, romping and skipping towards them, gathering round the visitors. They snickered and brayed, curled their lips and smiled toothy smiles, hoping for treats.

'Dad, bring your camera, quick!' Helen spotted the foal twins amongst the crowd. 'These two are so sweet!'

Click – click – click! David Moore took expert shots. A black donkey played to the camera. He rolled on to his back and kicked his legs in the air. Two small brown fillies with soft furry coats sidled up to the wall and rolled their big brown eyes. *Click – click!*

'Aah, look!' Hannah saw the twins fold their skinny legs like deckchairs and sink to the ground. They sat among the buttercups side by side, waiting for the fuss to die down.

'Hop in there,' Mr Moore told Hannah and Helen. 'I can get a good shot of the pair of you kneeling by the tiny ones. A picture like this should melt the hardest heart!'

Helen nipped into the field and sank down

beside the nearest foal. She rested her head against his soft neck and felt him cuddle up. Hannah put her arm round the other one. They all looked up at the camera.

'Perfect!' Mr Moore was balancing on the wall. He clicked away, then jumped into the field and crouched down to take more shots.

The twins turned away. Now they had eyes only for the baby donkeys, with their soft white noses and long pointed ears. When Hannah glanced up again, she was surprised to see the other donkeys backing off.

'Er, Da-ad!' Helen saw what the trouble was. One donkey was charging downhill with a certain look in his eye. He was a young, reddish-brown colt with a black mane standing stiff and proud, a black tail streaming behind him. And his hooves thundered towards them.

David Moore looked over his shoulder. He saw the donkey charging down at them, leapt heroically to his feet and put out his arms to stop him. 'Run!' he told the girls.

'Da-ad!' Helen closed her eyes.

Hannah froze. 'Too late!'

The brown donkey kicked and bucked. He skidded to a halt, face to face with their father. Then he pushed his nose towards him and grabbed the camera strap between his teeth. David Moore yelled and pulled. 'Oh no you don't!' He pulled so hard that the donkey let go and the twins' dad landed in a heap on the ground.

'Come on!' Hannah cried.

They ran to the rescue. Just as the donkey reared up, they pulled their dad sideways. The flailing hooves landed with a thud in the soft earth.

'This way!' Helen headed for the drive.

Together they stumbled and ran for safety, while the angry donkey kicked out at thin air.

'Quick!' Hannah vaulted over the white fence. Helen followed. Last of all came their dad, panting and puffing, swearing and gasping, through two bars of the fence. Just in time. The donkey had decided to make a second charge.

'I say,' a woman's voice shouted as they backed up the gravel drive towards the house. 'Are you all right? I saw him kicking up a fuss from the lounge window, and I thought I'd better get down here to sort him out!'

The Moores didn't dare to take their eyes off the charging donkey. It looked as if he was going to tear straight through the fence.

'Stand!' The woman gave a loud command.

The donkey heard and faltered. His gallop became a trot.

'Stand!'

He pulled up and dug his heels into the ground. Eyes rolling, nostrils blowing, he came to a full stop.

'Phew!' David Moore wiped a hand across his forehead.

The twins turned to look at the woman who had saved them. She strode down the hill in wellingtons and a green jacket, her curly grey hair blowing in the breeze. She was tall, with grey eyes to match her hair, and a suntanned face.

'Dorothy Miller!' she said, stretching out a hand to be shaken. 'But call me Dotty. Dotty by name, Dotty by nature!' Her voice boomed out, she shook hands firmly with them each in turn.

'That donkey gave us a nasty moment,' the twins' dad confessed, as they stood back rubbing the hands that had been shaken in Dotty Miller's strong grip.

She nodded. 'Sorry about that.' She tipped her head in the donkey's direction. 'He's new here. I brought him over from Ireland earlier this week.'

Helen and Hannah ventured towards the fence hard on the heels of the sanctuary's owner. She studied the donkey. He glared back at her, nostrils flared, mane bristling like a hoodlum with a Mohican haircut.

'What's his name?' Hannah asked, fascinated.

At first Dotty Miller didn't answer. 'He's a three-year-old, and I'm finding it difficult to settle him down. He's a fine donkey, but it's his temperament I'm not happy about.'

The donkey shifted from foot to foot. He raised his head and brayed long and loud.

'Meet Stevie,' Dotty said. She shook her head, sighed and led them up to the house. 'I don't know what I'm going to do with him. He's a rebel, and there's no two ways about it!'

Two

Spring Bank Holiday weekend in Doveton was one of the busiest times of the year. Tourists flocked to the lake to enjoy the boats and the windsurfing. Brave kids swam in the cold, clear water, while their sensible parents sat on the pebbly beach and dozed in the sun.

'Let's get these posters made up as soon as we can,' David Moore told the twins.

They'd gone home from Dotty Miller's place the night before, and worked in the dark-room, developing the films and printing the photographs of her donkeys.

Hannah agreed. 'We can take them round the shops and cafes. If people stick them in the window this weekend, Miss Miller will get lots of people to come to her Open Day.'

'When is it?' Helen cut and stuck the photographs on to big sheets of paper.

'Next Sunday.' Hannah wrote the message under the photographs:

LAKE VIEW DONKEY SANCTUARY
OPEN DAY
Sunday, 10.30 am–4.30 pm
Everyone welcome

'Your mum took some posters to work with her this morning,' their dad told them. 'She thinks a lot of visitors will drive over from Nesfield to see the donkeys, so it's worth putting posters up in the cafe.'

Mary Moore ran The Curlew Cafe in the busy town, while David Moore worked as a photographer from Home Farm. They all wanted to help Dotty Miller find good homes for her animals.

'Take a look at this one!' Helen held up one of the photographs which they'd developed the previous evening. 'It's Stevie. I'd know him anywhere!'

Hannah stopped writing and glanced across. The donkey glared out of the picture, head down, top lip curled back. 'He does look pretty mad.'

'Let me see.' Their dad pushed his wavy brown hair out of his eyes and leaned over their shoulders. 'It's like one of those mug-shots from an old cowboy film on TV! "Wanted: Dead or Alive!" '

The twins grinned. Stevie did look big, bad and ugly. 'Who'd want to give *him* a home?' Hannah wondered.

Helen stuck Stevie's photograph on to a poster. 'Maybe someone will,' she insisted.

They finished their work and got ready to take the posters into the village on their bikes. Bank Holiday meant traffic; cars nose to tail all the way over from Nesfield, crowds of daytrippers by the lake. David Moore preferred to leave the car in the yard and stay at home in the peace and quiet.

So Helen and Hannah set off down the lane, past Fred Hunt's farm at High Hartwell, and their schoolfriend Sam Lawson's home at Crackpot Farm. As expected, by the time they reached the big gates of Doveton Manor, the road was blocked with cars, and the pavements were spilling over with people in summer dresses, or T-shirts and shorts, peering into the craft-shop windows or eating ice-creams from Luke Martin's shop.

'Let's give Luke a couple of posters,' Helen suggested. 'He can put one inside, and one in the window.'

So they leaned their bikes against the lamp-post, then squeezed past the queue for ice-lollies and soft drinks. Knowing Luke was busy, the twins' plan was to quietly show him the posters and offer to stick them up themselves.

But a loud voice waylaid them. 'I say, it's the Moore girls, isn't it?' Dotty Miller hailed them from inside the shop.

All eyes turned and all ears tuned in to their conversation.

'Oh, very good, I see you've brought the posters for the Open Day! The more the merrier, eh?' She seized one from Hannah and unrolled it on the counter-top. 'Here's Carrie! A very good likeness.

She's a yearling. Good pedigree, lovely temperament!'

Several customers craned their heads to sneak a look. There were 'oohs' and 'aahs' all round.

'That one's made a hit,' Luke said, in between serving cheese and onion crisps and cola. 'Let's have it in the window.'

Hannah obliged with sellotape and scissors. Soon Carrie's big almond-shaped eyes stared down at the queue outside the door.

'Sweet!'

'Adorable!'

'Wouldn't you just love to take that one home?'

Hannah grinned at Helen, while Dotty sorted through the posters. 'Cathleen, Simon, Hamlet, Sooty . . .' She named each donkey on the photos. 'Sooty's getting on in years, he's a bit long in the tooth, but he's a very loving old chap.'

'Put him up on the notice-board,' Luke said with a smile, as he gave change for chocolate and orange juice.

'Excellent!' Dotty boomed, as this time Helen got to work with the drawing-pins. She picked up the newspaper which she'd come to the village to buy. 'At this rate we'll have a nice big crowd at Lake View next Sunday!' She buttoned up her shabby green jacket, ready to squeeze out of the shop.

But her eye fell on one of the posters that Hannah was rolling up to put back into her bag. 'Oh, I say!' She pulled it towards her. 'That one looks a bit grim!'

People peered again and murmured with surprise. Stevie glared out at them with his bristling mane and bared teeth.

'I don't think we should use this picture to advertise our donkeys!'

'He does look a bit of a bruiser,' Luke agreed.

'I quite like him, actually.' Helen blushed as she spoke. She hadn't meant to stick up for the bad-tempered donkey; it just slipped out. 'He's got character.'

Dotty Miller frowned. She waited for Hannah to pack up the posters, then drew them both outside. Once they were safely out of earshot, she went into more detail. 'I didn't like to say any more in there, but I'm afraid it won't be easy to find a home for Stevie.'

'Why not?' Hannah wondered what else had happened.

'After you left yesterday, he got into all sorts of trouble, kicking and bullying the other donkeys. He's so much bigger than some of them; over eleven hands. And this mean streak is quite a problem. He went for poor old Sooty, who's never done any harm to anyone, and gave him a nasty kick. In the end, I had to put Stevie in solitary confinement, away from the rest. He's in a paddock at the back of the house. I've called in the vet to take a look at him, just in case there's a problem that's making him so bad-tempered.'

Helen and Hannah pricked up their ears. Stevie's reputation grew worse by the minute, but they were interested. He might kick and nip and bully, but deep down they were sure there must be a friendly donkey wanting to get out.

'Erm, would you mind if we, um, sort of, came and watched?' Helen hardly knew Dotty Miller. She stuttered out the question that both she and Hannah were thinking.

'Of course not!' The answer shot out like a bullet. 'Any time. Come when you want. Sally Freeman's due at eleven. Biscuits and orange juice ready and waiting!' With that, Miss Miller strode to her car and set off.

Hannah took a deep breath. 'Are we sure about this?' Helen had jumped in with both feet and invited themselves up to Lake View.

Helen nodded. 'I feel sorry for Stevie, don't you?'

'I suppose so.'

'He can't have been *born* bad, can he? Something must have made him that way.

Hannah agreed. 'I suppose his last owners treated him badly. Or maybe it's something else, and Mrs Freeman will be able to find out what's wrong.' She hesitated. 'The thing is, it's Miss Miller . . .'

'What about her?' Helen was ready to cycle off after the vanishing car.

'She's a bit, kind of, scary! Her voice barks at you, and she strides everywhere in her wellies and jacket, just like an army sergeant!'

Helen shrugged. 'Never mind her. It's Stevie we're interested in.' Helen never let minor details put her off. 'Come on, let's go!'

And Hannah didn't want Helen to think she'd turned weedy. She sat astride her bike and set off first, along the crowded Main Street, up the hill towards Lake View.

Three

'Trouble with a capital "T"!' Dotty Miller told Sally Freeman when she turned up at Lake View with her vet's bag. 'From the minute he stepped out of the horse box on Wednesday, he's been lashing out at anything that moves.'

Helen and Hannah watched the vet get to work. They stood behind the paddock fence as Miss Miller called out a command for Stevie to stand still. The donkey seemed to quiver with annoyance, but he stood warily as Mrs Freeman approached.

She walked slowly up to him, talking softly as she

went. 'Good boy! There's a good boy. We're not going to hurt you.' She turned to Miss Miller. 'Can we tie him up?'

'No, he won't let me anywhere near him, as a matter of fact. I've tried to put a halter on him, but no luck!'

'Hmm. Nobody's taken any care at all of you, have they?' She spoke to the donkey again. 'I wonder where you came from, and who treated you so badly?' Her calm voice seemed to quieten Stevie. He stopped quivering and let the vet reach out to pat his neck.

'See!' Helen whispered to Hannah. 'I knew he couldn't be all bad.'

'What's she looking for?' Hannah asked Miss Miller, as the vet gently lifted one of Stevie's front legs and examined the hoof.

'Seedy toe, laminitis, mud fever . . .' the strange-sounding answers rapped out short and sharp. 'Or it could be ringworm, or sweet itch; all kinds of parasites might make him bad-tempered.'

They watched as Sally checked Stevie's legs one by one, then his head, his ears, his belly and his back end.

'He *is* being good!' Hannah whispered back to Helen.

'Because she's being nice to him,' Helen pointed out. They could hear Mrs Freeman telling Stevie what a good boy he was all the time she worked. 'He trusts her.'

'She's coming over!' Hannah stood on the fence to hear the verdict.

Sally Freeman's face gave nothing away as she patted the donkey's neck and told him to walk on. Then she came to speak to Miss Miller.

'I can't see anything,' she said in the same low

voice she'd used with the donkey. 'I've given him a thorough examination, and as far as I can judge he's a perfectly healthy three-year-old.'

Helen joined Hannah on the fence. She frowned.

Dotty Miller pursed her lips. 'Life is never that simple, eh?'

'I'm afraid not. If there had been a problem with his health, it could very well account for his bad behaviour, and we could have cleared it up pretty quickly. But it's not that.'

Hannah noticed that Stevie had trotted off to the far side of the paddock. His ears were pricked, as if he was listening to something she couldn't pick up.

'It goes deeper, then.' Even Dotty Miller lowered her voice to discuss Stevie's problem. 'That's a pity.'

'Yes, it means he'll need a lot of time and tender loving care to put him right. I wouldn't trust him with an inexperienced owner at present.' She took her car keys out of her pocket, then climbed over the fence to join them.

'He can't be that bad.' Helen protested. 'Everyone was painting a black picture of Stevie. 'Maybe he'll be OK once he's settled down!'

'Oh, wait a sec, I've forgotten my hoof-pick.'

Sally Freeman looked back into the paddock.

'I'll get it!' Helen volunteered and scrambled over the fence before anyone could stop her.

Across the paddock, Stevie turned and stamped his foot. Hannah saw his ears go back as he lowered his head and glared. 'You'd better be quick!' she called to Helen.

Helen had crouched down to look for the hoof-pick, so she didn't see Stevie set off across the field. His trot turned into a gallop, he was heading full tilt towards her.

'Watch out!' Hannah gripped the fence and yelled.

'Stand!' Miss Miller bellowed at the charging donkey.

'Quick, Helen, get out of here!' Mrs Freeman jumped the fence to distract Stevie from Helen's crouching figure.

But the donkey was dead set on turfing Helen out of his paddock. He charged straight at her, hooves thudding, teeth bared. She turned and jumped up. For a second she froze with fear.

'Run, Helen!' Hannah cried. To add to the confusion, a car had driven up the drive with a roar

and a screech of brakes. Now it sounded its horn
from the front of the house.

Helen ran. She dodged sideways, out of the way

of the flying hooves, just out of reach of Stevie's snapping teeth. But she was close enough to see his wild eyes, to feel his hot breath on her face. Then she felt Sally Freeman grab her arm and haul her towards the fence. Soon they were safely on the outside, while Stevie reared up and pawed the air.

'That was close!' Hannah breathed a sigh of relief. 'I don't know what got into him!' A minute earlier, after Mrs Freeman had examined him, Stevie had seemed fine. Now he was lashing out at everything in sight.

'Wait a moment while I see who's kicking up that fuss out front.' Miss Miller stomped off to deal with the noisy car driver who was still blaring his horn. She disappeared round the front of the house.

'Are you OK?' Mrs Freeman asked Helen.

'Fine, thanks.' Her legs felt shaky from shock, and she was breathing hard. Otherwise there was no harm done. 'I didn't expect that, though.' By now, Stevie had reeled away and charged across the paddock.

'It confirms what Dotty said about him, at any rate.' The vet helped to dust Helen down. 'Trouble with a capital "T"!' Before she left, she warned them not to go inside the paddock again.

'No way!' Hannah agreed. She stared at the bucking donkey as he careered around the field.

'Once is enough.' Helen choked, catching her breath.

But they did stay to watch, long after the grown-ups had gone and the sound of two cars disappearing down the drive told them that Miss Miller had dealt with the horn blower and was in the house alone.

'Let's face it, he's a rebel,' Hannah said slowly.

Helen didn't reply.

'It's more than just taking a while to settle down in his new home.'

Silence.

'He's got a wild streak.'

Stevie reared and kicked, as if to prove the point.

'And there's nothing anyone can do about it.'

Helen narrowed her dark brown eyes and pushed her fringe away from her face. Stevie had turned and had them in his sights again. He raised his head and brayed. 'Nothing anyone can do about it, eh?' she repeated. 'Well, I don't know about that. We'll just have to wait and see!'

Four

'All you need is love,' David Moore hummed a famous tune. '*Da-da da-da dum*!' He served breakfast on a fine Bank Holiday Monday.

'Don't tease,' Mary Moore warned him. 'The girls are probably right. This donkey is probably only mean because someone's mistreated him.' She wound her long dark hair on to the top of her head, ready to set off for work at The Curlew. 'Do you know where he came from?'

Helen shook her head. She sat at the kitchen table, resting her feet on Speckle's back. Every so often she fed him a scrap of her breakfast. 'Only

31

that he came over from Ireland.'

'The funny thing is, he was OK with Mrs Freeman,' Hannah pointed out. The twins had spent all last evening trying to work out what was wrong with the donkey.

'He's a natural delinquent,' their dad had warned them, after he overheard them discussing Stevie in the barn while they groomed Solo.

'What does that mean?' Hannah had brushed with all her might. Solo's back was gleaming.

'Wild, untameable, born to be bad,' he said in a low American drawl. 'It's in his genes.'

Helen had raised her eyebrows. 'Jeans?'

'No, *genes*. You know; he's inherited his wild streak from his parents. Like you, Helen!'

She gave him a shove with her elbow. 'It's your fault, then! Anyway, I don't believe it.'

'Is there such a thing as a donkey who can't be tamed?' Hannah asked her mum now. Mary Moore had grown up in the country, and knew more about animals than their dad.

'I don't know. Donkeys are supposed to be friendly and clever. The people next door to us had one because he was safer with small children than a pony.' She bent to give the girls a quick peck on the cheek. 'But I guess there's the odd one who turns mean.'

'The *very* odd one,' David Moore cut in.

'Anyway, I have to go to work.' She patted Speckle and kissed their dad goodbye.

'Did you put the Open Day posters up in the cafe?' Hannah reminded her.

'Yep. Lots of people seemed interested, too.'

'Thanks, Mum.'

'Be good.'

'Fat chance.' Their dad was suspicious. 'Why aren't you eating your breakfast, Hannah? What are you up to?'

'Not hungry. Nothing.' Hannah sounded vague. Her mum was hardly out of the door, and already she was off in a world of her own.

Helen slipped Speckle her last scrap of scrambled egg. She bit her lip and leaned her elbow on the table, deep in thought. 'It's a bit like a boy who skives school really, isn't it?'

'What is?' Their dad was still mystified.

'Stevie. Usually, if a kid gets into trouble, there's a reason; like his mum and dad have split up, or he's being bullied, or whatever.'

'This is too deep for me,' Mr Moore protested, clearing the plates from the table. 'What's a bad-tempered donkey got to do with divorce?'

'I mean, there's a reason!' To Helen it was perfectly clear.

'Yes, and you wouldn't just give up on a kid who's in trouble, would you?' Hannah backed her sister. 'You'd want to do something to help.'

'Uh-oh!' Their dad clicked. 'Why do I feel another adoption plan coming on?' Every time the twins found an animal in trouble, they sprang to the rescue. They had Speckle and Solo, Sunny, and Socks, the kitten, who had just strolled into the kitchen to find a warm spot beside the stove. Then they had Snip and Snap, the goat kids, adopted from Fred Hunt's farm. Home Farm was practically bursting at the seams.

'No-oh!' Helen protested. 'Who said we wanted to adopt Stevie?'

'You usually do.'

'We only want to find out a bit more about him,' Hannah explained. 'That's why we thought we might go over to Lake View this morning.' They hadn't discussed it, but she knew what was in Helen's mind.

'Right!' Helen sprang up. 'That's it. We want to find out what's made him the way he is!'

'Hmm, and I was born yesterday!'

'It's OK, Dad. We won't go near him.' Hannah put on her sensible voice.

'And you're sure Dotty Miller doesn't mind?'

'No. She gives us biscuits and orange juice.' Never mind that the biscuits were stale and the juice was watery. Never mind that Miss Miller still scared them stiff with her rattling voice and frizzy hair.

'Oh, OK.' David Moore gave in. 'Just so long as you don't try to reform this donkey. I wouldn't want you to get your hopes up or anything.'

'Would we?' Helen said modestly, rushing for the door.

'Of course not.' Hannah followed. 'Even Miss Miller sees him as a challenge. What on earth could we do that she can't?' When she wanted to be, Hannah was sweet reason itself.

'I never heard of children turning down custard

creams before!' Dotty Miller closed the tin with surprise.

Helen smiled. 'We've just had breakfast, thanks.' Glad to escape the soggy biscuits, the twins followed the sanctuary owner out of the house. Stopping at the stable in the yard to collect nets of hay, they went down into the donkey field.

'Only the best hay, of course,' Miss Miller told them. 'I buy it from John Fox at Lakeside Farm. You love it, don't you, Damson?'

A purplish grey donkey came trotting to the fence, followed by half a dozen others. Dotty slung the haynets over a post, and soon all that could be heard was the happy sound of teeth munching through crisp hay.

'Do you give them *all* names?' Hannah asked. Two of the donkeys found her T-shirt more interesting than the hay. They came and nibbled at it, thrusting their noses at her and snuffling for a treat.

'Every single one. They're individuals, you see. Damson here is a gentle donkey. She loves to be with people. And Sooty likes to help. He'll carry panniers or pull firewood in a cart. Whereas

Cathleen there is a little bit lazy and spoiled. But on the whole, they're affectionate animals, and not at all stubborn, as some people think.'

Helen watched the contented scene. 'So why is Stevie different?'

It was the burning question that they'd come to find out the answer to. Poor Stevie was still in solitary confinement, heard but not seen. His bad-tempered bray tore through the air as the other donkeys came to chat.

'Well, we don't know his story exactly.' Miss Miller was busy inspecting ears and mouths, then popping in a carrot treat as a reward. Helen and Hannah followed quietly. 'He's from County Cork in Ireland; we know that much. A good looker; nice neat head, long neck, straight back. That means his pedigree is fine.'

'But?' Hannah prompted.

'But take a look at his eye when you get the chance. A donkey's eye should be large and kind, like Carrie's here. I needed only one quick look at Stevie's eye to realise he would be trouble. Come and see.' She turned and led the way up the hill.

'How does that happen?'

'Who knows? Perhaps he's been passed from one owner to another without anyone to really care. It's even possible that he's been actively mistreated. And a donkey is an intelligent creature. He won't obey an order just because you tell him to. He has to see some sense in it. A stupid owner can ruin him.'

Hannah nodded. 'Poor Stevie.'

'How did he end up at Lake View if he lived in Ireland?' Helen asked. They went round the side of the house to find Stevie in his small paddock.

'I'm afraid he'd done the rounds of the donkey homes over there, and they all found him too hard to handle. I got to hear about him and decided to give him one last chance.' Miss Miller stopped by the fence, hands in pockets, listening to Stevie's racket as he thundered round his prison. 'The crux of the matter is trust,' she frowned.

'What do you mean?' Helen and Hannah asked in the same split second. Stevie had seen them and stood stock still, glaring at them with suspicion. He was in the shadow of a beech tree; a dark, angry creature ready to strike out at anyone who came near.

'If a donkey trusts you, he'll be your friend for ever. But how do we win that trust? There's the problem.'

Hannah and Helen thought they might have an answer, but they weren't ready to give it yet. They stared silently across the paddock.

'And, of course, eventually we need to find a new home for him,' she continued. 'Somewhere where he'll be well looked after for the rest of his long life. But he's so cantankerous, I'm afraid we won't find anyone to take him on.'

Again the twins were silent. But they looked at each other with a gleam in their eyes.

Dotty Miller sighed and shook her head. 'After all, who will be willing to give him a home when he's so stubborn and ready to bite the hand that feeds him?'

Five

'How come this pig finds so much mud to roll in on a sunny day like today?' David Moore had his sleeves rolled up and a stiff brush in his hand.

Hannah and Helen had got back from Lake View and gone into the barn to find him. They wanted to tell him the sad story of poor Stevie.

Sunny oinked at them.

'And never mind oinking,' their dad warned him. 'No one's going to feel sorry for you just because you're being forced to have a wash!'

The sturdy piglet oinked again. In the corner of the barn Speckle sat lazily wagging his tail at the twins, while little Socks lay curled up at his side.

Mr Moore took up a big bucket of foaming, soapy water and put it on a bench. 'Bathtime for you, mate!' He got to work scrubbing the dirt off a wriggling Sunny.

The twins enjoyed the show.

'You missed a bit!' Helen pointed to a lump of mud behind Sunny's right ear.

'Watch it, Dad, there's soap on his nose. He's about to . . . sneeze!' Hannah tried to warm him.

Sunny screwed up his face and gave a great *atchoo*! David Moore leaped back in surprise and stumbled against the bucket. It tipped, wobbled, and spilled. All over their dad's jeans! He stood soaked to the skin.

Helen and Hannah roared with laughter. The piglet was only half-washed and their dad was drenched.

'Wait here. I'll fetch a towel,' Hannah said. She ran into the house.

'I'll finish cleaning Sunny up and make him look decent,' Helen offered. She took the stiff brush and began to scrub off the rest of the dirt. The piglet sighed with pleasure.

Dripping and squelching, their dad retreated into the yard and waited for Hannah to come running back with the towel. As she handed it to him, she switched the subject. 'Miss Miller told us a lot about donkeys this morning,' she said. 'I never knew they were related to zebras.'

'Yes, I suppose they are.' He was so busy drying himself down that he didn't suspect where Hannah was leading.

'And they're very, very intelligent.'

'That's what you said about pigs,' he reminded her.

A false move, she realised. Quickly she went on. 'Miss Miller says that could be why Stevie has so many problems.'

'What? Nobody understands him because he's super-clever?' He gave her a funny look.

Hannah blew her fringe up from her sticky forehead. This conversation wasn't going the right way. Still she persevered. 'In a way. Anyway, she says she can't risk putting him back in with the other donkeys. He needs to be by himself until he learns to calm down. And it turns out she can't find the space. She needs the paddock to train the rest and get them ready for the Open Day.'

David Moore took off one of his squelchy trainers and tipped it upside down. Water trickled on to the yard. 'What will she do; send him back where he came from?'

'She can't. His old owners in Ireland don't want him back.'

'Maybe somebody will be daft enough to give him a home on Sunday, then.' Off came his other trainer.

'Miss Miller says she doesn't think she can even keep him *that* long.'

There was a pause while more water trickled down. 'Uh-oh!' Her dad looked up. 'N-O, no!'

At that moment, Helen came out of the barn with Sunny, Speckle and Socks. They stood listening in the doorway.

'What? I never even asked!' Hannah protested, her face all innocence.

'No, but you were just about to. Think about it, Hannah. Think what chaos a stubborn donkey would cause here at Home Farm! He'd be up to his crazy tricks, kicking and nipping and pinching. What about the other animals? What about Solo and Speckle? What about Socks and Snip and Snap? What about poor defenceless little Sunny here?'

Hannah opened her eyes wide. Helen's mouth fell open.

'And before you try to get around me, think about your mother. She already has too much on her hands, running the cafe and helping to take care of this place. You don't want her to have any more on her plate, do you?'

Helen frowned. 'Clever!' she grunted. Their dad was good at making them feel guilty.

There was no answer to this. Hannah was lost for words.

'No, no,' their dad went on. 'It wouldn't be fair even to ask.'

'But what about Stevie?' Helen had one last go. 'What's going to happen to him?'

'That's not our problem. Remember, you can't solve all the troubles in the world, and this is one that Dotty Miller has to sort out for herself. She brought the donkey over, and now she's stuck with him. I must say, I don't envy her; who in their right mind would want to take Stevie home with them? Take one look at him, and most people would run a mile!' Grumbling and shaking his head, David Moore went inside to change his trousers.

'Bad timing,' Helen told Hannah.

Hannah screwed her mouth up and gave a loud sigh. She glanced at the row of obedient animals sitting waiting for a signal from her, then she pictured Stevie barging in here and running riot. 'You don't think Dad's got a point, do you?' she asked faintly.

Helen glared. She gave Hannah one of her scornful looks, before she turned on her heel and stormed off towards Solo's field.

'No, obviously not!' Hannah sighed, as she bent to pick up Socks and cuddle him. Everyone was arguing and getting cross, all because of Stevie.

For the rest of the day they did their own thing, thought their own thoughts, but came up with no answer to what was turning out to be one of the trickiest questions they'd had to face since the Moore family had came to live at Home Farm.

Mary Moore arrived home exhausted. She sank into an armchair and kicked off her shoes. 'If I ever see another toasted teacake, I'll scream!'

Hannah and Helen took her bag, brought her a footstool, a cup of tea, her favourite magazine. With Socks on her lap and Speckle snuggled under her stool, she soon revived.

'Busy day?' Hannah asked.

'Crazy. I thought we were going to run out of everything. I've never seen such crowds in Nesfield. What about you? What did you do?'

'Not much.' Hannah had made up her mind not to mention Stevie. Their dad was right; it wasn't fair to their mum, and probably not fair to the other animals either.

Mary looked hard from Hannah to Helen and back again. 'Does "not much" include paying a visit to the donkey home?'

Hannah shrugged, Helen sighed. She too was doing her best not to talk about 'The Problem'.

'How was Dotty? Is everything ready for next Sunday?'

'She was fine,' Hannah said, her voice flat.

'Hmm.' Their mum sipped her tea. The hall clock ticked.

'I was just thinking . . . !'

'Actually, we were wondering . . . !'

47

'There *was* one thing . . . !'

Mary, Helen and Hannah spoke at once. They each stopped to let the others go first.

'I was just thinking about that poor donkey you told me about.' Mrs Moore smiled and went on calmly.

'Stevie!' Helen got in first.

'Stevie!' Hannah echoed.

'Yes, it's been bothering me all day. I was remembering the sweet little donkey that the family next door to me had when I was a girl. His name was Daniel, and they could do anything with him. They even took him to the shops!'

The girls knew when not to interrupt. Instead, they sat on the floor and drew their knees up under their chins, hugging their legs as she went on.

'They used to say that what a donkey likes best is company. If you leave them in a field by themselves, they get bored and lonely. Just like people, I suppose.'

Socks curled up sleepily and waved her paws in the air. Speckle put his chin on Mrs Moore's lap.

'A donkey would get plenty of company here at

Home Farm, wouldn't he?' she murmured.

'Solo and Sunny would keep an eye on him out in the field, and there's always Snip and Snap, and the hens and the rabbits too . . .' Mary turned her head and blew the twins' dad a kiss. He'd come down from his dark-room and followed the sound of voices into the lounge. 'What do you think; is there enough room for him here?' she asked.

'Who's "him"?' He came and leaned over the back of her chair, stroking her tired forehead.

'What's-his-name, the rebel donkey.'

'Stevie!' the twins cried again, their eyes alight.

'Yes. Wouldn't it be nice to offer him somewhere to live?' she said.

'*Nice*!' David Moore shot upright.

Helen and Hannah leaped to their feet. 'Oh, Mum, it would be fantastic! . . . We'd look after him really well! . . . He'd soon settle down! . . . Oh . . . oh . . . oh, brilliant!' They jumped and hugged, and cavorted around the room.

Speckle barked, Socks woke up and stole out of the door. David Moore looked stunned.

'Just hold on a darned minute!' he drawled.

'I know; it's a big responsibility,' Mary smiled. She went and put her arms round his neck. 'And we wouldn't go ahead if you didn't want to . . .'

The twins fell silent, they held their breaths.

David Moore stared at their pleading faces.

'We never said a word, Dad, honest!' Helen said.

'It was Mum's idea!' Hannah insisted.

'It was,' Mary Moore agreed. 'I have this picture of a soppy, loveable donkey to keep me company in my old age, when the girls have left home, and it's just the two of us here in this big old house.'

'A *loveable* donkey; yes!' He hesitated. The

twins saw he was weakening. 'But does it have to be *this* one?'

Mary turned to the girls. They gave the smallest, tiniest nods. She turned back to their dad.

'I must be mad,' he groaned.

'Does that mean you agree?'

'Completely crazy.' He nodded.

It was all Hannah and Helen needed. They whooped and danced, ran out into the yard, told anyone who would listen. 'Stevie is coming to live at Home Farm!' they yelled at the rabbits and the hens. 'It was Mum's idea. We didn't even have to ask!'

Dotty Miller brought him over first thing next morning. Her horse box swayed and rattled up Doveton Fell into the farmyard, just as the mists were rising and a pale sun breaking through the clouds.

'Here he comes!' Helen ran out of the house to meet him, followed by Hannah, and their mum and dad.

Miss Miller jumped down from her Land Rover and strode across to shake hands. 'Awfully good of you!' she beamed. 'To take on such a handful, I mean!'

Inside the box, the donkey kicked and threw himself against the metal sides.

'Gets me out of a tight spot, I must say; what with the Open Day coming up and all that!' As she took a deep, healthy breath, her big chest heaved up and down. 'Mind you, I hope you realise what you've taken on.'

Stevie beat his hooves on the floor and brayed for all he was worth. The chickens in the farmyard crept inside the barn, while Socks slunk into the house. Only Speckle stood his ground as the noise went on.

'It's going to take an awful lot of hard work to lick him into shape.' She wanted them to know how difficult it would be to train him. 'The iron's already entered his soul, if you know what I mean.'

'But he's only young,' Mary Moore pointed out. Her face was looking worried as she saw the horse box rock to and fro. 'Surely he just needs firm handling and kindness?'

'Let's hope so.' Dotty refused to meet her gaze. 'Where do you want him; inside or out?'

'In the barn,' Helen suggested. 'We've put down fresh straw, and Hannah made up a haynet. He can use Solo's stall until he settles down.'

So Miss Miller got into the Land Rover and backed the box up to the barn door. Then she came round to unbolt the ramp. 'Stand back,' she warned. 'I'll have to open the door a bit at a time and let him get his bearings.'

Slowly she eased the bolts free and looked round. 'Ready?'

David Moore stood with his arm around Mary's shoulder. They kept well back from the horse box, heeding Dotty's warning. Helen and Hannah stood at the far side, craning to see.

'Here goes!' Miss Miller opened the door and stood back.

As soon as the fresh air hit him, Stevie let loose. He pounded the floor of the horse box, then lurched forwards down the ramp. He stumbled and half fell, then was up on his feet, bucking and kicking. His hooves flashed. They caught the horse box with a loud crash, then flailed into thin air. He wheeled and kicked out at the wall and the barn door. The thuds sent Speckle crouching into a corner of the yard.

'Leave him!' Dotty said quietly, as Helen and

Hannah made as if to move towards the donkey.

Stevie's eyes rolled, his nostrils flared as he tossed his head. At last he skittered sideways into the barn.

'Close the doors!' Dotty ordered.

The twins moved swiftly to obey. Soon the barn doors were bolted and Stevie was safe on the inside.

'Don't try to go near until he gets used to his new surroundings.'

'How long will that be?' The twins' father wanted to know. His face was grim.

'Well, he can't keep up this racket for ever. Give him a few hours to calm down, then try him with a bucket of water. He's bound to be thirsty. And give me a ring if you need any more advice.' Miss Miller had swung up into the driver's seat and was leaning out of the open window. 'If the worst comes to the worst, I can always come and take him back to Lake View!'

'Oh no, we'll be OK, thanks,' Helen said. But her heart quaked as she heard those hooves thudding and crashing inside the barn.

'Yes, fine,' Hannah agreed. *Poor thing*, she

thought as she listened to the donkey's frightened squeals. *It's dark in there, and he's all alone!*

Mr and Mrs Moore said nothing. Dotty Miller backed her Land Rover out into the lane and drove off.

Even Helen wondered where on earth they were going to start. She gazed at the bolted doors, heard the anger behind the donkey's crashing hooves. 'Welcome to Home Farm!' she whispered.

Six

'We have to plan a campaign,' Helen decided. She sat with Hannah on the kitchen doorstep, trying to work out what to do.

'You make it sound like a war,' Hannah sighed. Why couldn't kind words and treats do the trick?

'It is. It's a battle of wills between him and us!'

'Who says?'

'It's obvious. Stevie has to know we mean what we say, otherwise he'll get away with murder. But we don't need to be cruel.' She pushed her hair behind her ears and opened a notebook. 'Day One: Teach Stevie Command Words.' She wrote as she spoke, then underlined the heading. 'Which command words does he need to learn first?'

' "Stand",' Hannah suggested. She remembered that this was the word that Miss Miller had used. 'And how about "No!"?'

Helen jotted them down. 'Then there's "Walk" and "Trot".'

'I don't think we'll get as far as that on Day One.' After a couple of hours in the barn, Stevie was quieter, but they could still hear him kicking out every now and then. Sheer tiredness seemed to have calmed him down, however. 'When do we start?'

'This afternoon.' Helen was brisk. 'If he does something we like, we say "Good boy!". If it's something bad, we say "No!". OK?'

Hannah nodded. 'But we don't have to shout, do we? It can be "No!" in a quiet voice, but still meaning it.' She felt worried that Stevie wouldn't like being yelled at.

' "No", quiet but firm,' Helen agreed and wrote it down. 'The first thing is to get him to wear a halter. Remember, Miss Miller said she couldn't get one on him.'

'We'll use Solo's.' Luckily they had all the tack they needed.

'Then he has to learn to walk forwards, backwards and to stop.'

'That's Day Two,' Hannah insisted. 'We can't hurry him, remember.'

'Then to trot, then go up and down steps and slopes and through narrow doorways.' Helen rushed on. 'And he has to learn to lift up his feet to have his hooves cleaned, and stand still to be groomed!'

Just then, Stevie let out a mighty kick against the wooden stall in the barn. The sound crashed around the farmyard. 'It's going to take ages!' Hannah sighed.

David Moore came and called them in for lunch. He'd promised their mother before she went off to work that he wouldn't let the twins do anything dangerous as far as Stevie was concerned. And all morning he'd warned them to leave the donkey alone in the barn. Now he agreed that he seemed to be quietening down.

'What's the plan of action?' he asked as he dished out the pizza.

'We're going to open the top half of the door and let him look out and see where he is,' Hannah told him. 'That'll be this afternoon.'

'Then later, we're going to talk nicely to him and see if we can fit a halter on him.' Helen ate quickly. 'Then we're going to lead him out into the yard.'

'If we get that far.' Hannah was nervous. She picked at her food and tried to picture how Stevie would react.

'Then what?'

'Then we teach him to walk and stand still, then we get him out into Solo's field, then the two of them make friends, and we train Stevie to walk and trot. Before long we'll be saddling him up and taking him out for rides!'

David Moore grunted. 'Easy-peasy!'

Helen blushed. 'We're on holiday all this week!' She'd finished her lunch and was raring to go. 'Come on, Hannah, come on, Speckle!' She grabbed a bucket from under the sink and took it to the outside tap to fill it up.

'One step at a time, remember!' Mr Moore insisted. 'I'll be working upstairs if you need me.'

'Thanks, Dad.' Hannah followed Helen out of the

house. This was it; Day One of Stevie's training programme was about to begin.

The donkey poked his head out of the door. The whites of his eyes showed as he stared at Helen and Hannah. His dark brown neck was covered in sweat.

'Good boy!' Helen approached quietly. She held the bucket of water and waited at a safe distance.

'That's it, good boy!' Hannah stood to one side.

Stevie snorted and tossed his head.

'This will cool you down,' Helen promised as she advanced with the bucket. She hung it on a hook by the door where the donkey could reach it. He watched every movement she made.

Patiently they waited for him to drink. He sniffed, then turned his head this way and that; nothing coming, no danger. So he lowered his head to the water.

'Goo-ood boy!' Helen was thrilled. 'That's better. You drink as much as you like. No one's going to stop you!' She spoke gently, with a soft lilt, soothing the poor donkey's raw nerves.

'He hated that horse box,' Hannah said quietly.

'I've never seen an animal as upset as that before.'

'Well, it's better now, and you'll never have to go in one of those horrid things again if you don't want to,' Helen promised.

Stevie finished the water and looked warily round the yard.

'See, no nasty horse box!' Hannah didn't blame him for panicking. To Stevie it must seem a frightening time, locked up inside a dark box with loud noises roaring by on the road. She glanced at Helen and allowed herself a quick smile. 'So far, so good,' she whispered.

They talked to Stevie, quietly getting to know him without trying to teach him anything. Once in a while, Mr Moore would pop out to see how they were getting on, then he would go back upstairs to work. Stevie would bridle if he came too near, but by teatime he would let both Helen and Hannah come up and gently stroke his neck.

'Miss Miller was wrong about one thing,' Hannah whispered. She was scratching the hard dome of Stevie's forehead and he was pushing against her hand, asking for more.

'What?' Helen had taken the halter off a hook by

the door and stood waiting for the right moment to slip it on.

'She talked about his eye. She said it wasn't a kind eye, remember?' In fact, Stevie's eyes were big and oval, and they shone a dark, dark brown. 'Well, it is,' Hannah told him. 'I think it's a lovely eye, and you're a beautiful boy!'

Helen moved forward with the halter, and it was done! She slipped the nylon webbing over his head and across his nose, then held on to the rope that went under his chin. 'Good boy!' She praised him and patted his nose, as Stevie jerked his head once, then accepted the halter.

It was time to open the bottom section of the door. Helen held Stevie firm while Hannah bent to loosen the bolts. The door swung open with a creak.

Would he move forward? Or would he back off in fright and begin to pull at the rope?

Helen held her wrist stiff and stood close to his side. She pointed him towards the yard.

'I'll take the bucket into the middle,' Hannah suggested, hoping that he would want to head for the refreshing drink.

Stevie kept his eye on her, but didn't move.

'Walk!' Helen said softly. She pushed him forward with her stiff wrist. 'Go on, walk – walk – walk!'

The donkey lifted his foot, but twisted his head away and pulled on the rope.

'No!' she said firmly.

He stopped twisting and took his first step.

'Good boy! Now walk!' She clicked her tongue to gee him up.

He took two more steps towards the bucket.

As Hannah watched, hardly daring to breathe, a smile spread slowly across her face. 'He's doing it!'

'Walk – walk – walk!' Helen encouraged him step by step towards Hannah and the bucket.

When he finally reached it, they could have flung their arms around his neck. Instead, Helen slackened her hold and let him lower his head to drink.

'Very good!' David Moore's voice called faintly from high above their heads.

The twins glanced up. There he was, his head poking out of the attic window where he had his dark-room. He'd been watching their first success!

They beamed up at him.

'So far, so good!' Hannah said again, running her fingers through Stevie's stiff black mane and patting his soft neck. 'Now let's see what else you can do!'

'He can walk, he can stand still when we tell him, and now he'll even let himself be tied up!' Helen described all the orders that Stevie had obeyed. It was late in the afternoon, and she and Hannah had worked hard.

'Well done.' David Moore looked on as Hannah hitched Stevie's halter rope around the gatepost. 'You must be exhausted.'

'So is Stevie.' Excitement bubbled inside her and stopped her from realising how tired she was. Everyone had said it was impossible to tame him, but now, in one afternoon, the twins had got him to trust them and do as they asked. 'We're going to give him a good feed, brush him down and put him to bed for the night.'

'Good for you.' He smiled and shook his head. 'Who would have believed it?'

'I know. It's brilliant, isn't it?' She left him and went across to join Hannah. 'Dad says well done.'

'You hear that? Well done!' Hannah patted Stevie's shoulder. He pulled a little at the rope attached to the post. 'No!' she said in her firm voice.

'He doesn't like being tied to that post much. Let's finish for the day,' Helen suggested. 'We can try tying him up again tomorrow. He'll soon get used to it.'

'Stand!' Hannah took hold of the rope to one side of the donkey's mouth. He grew restless as Helen unhitched rope from the post. 'No!' She didn't want him to pull and hurt himself. Once he had a bit and bridle on, the pulling would cut into his mouth.

But Stevie ignored the command. He went on skittering sideways, away from the gate.

A car was coming up the lane towards the farm, its engine growing louder. Stevie clattered his hooves on the stone flags and began to toss his head, while Hannah held on hard. 'It's OK, it's only Mum!' She recognised the sound. 'Whoa, boy!'

But her voice was lost in a terrific, angry bray; half scream, half bellow. Stevie wrenched the rope out of her hand and broke loose. Caught behind

him, Helen had to plunge out of the way of his flailing hooves.

David Moore ran to the door, and as Mary drove into the yard, the donkey was running wild. He charged the length of the farmyard, smashing flowerpots and trampling bushes as he went. He kicked out at the rabbit hutch, just missing it, and made the hens run squawking in all directions. Out of control, crazy again, he smashed against a shed door, winded himself and sank to his knees.

'What on earth . . . ?' Mary Moore jumped out and gazed at her ruined pots. Soil lay scattered across the yard, the tender plants were trampled to a pulp.

'Stevie!' All Hannah could do was gasp his name. Her wrist hurt where he'd pulled free, there were tears of disappointment in her eyes.

Helen gritted her teeth. Ignoring the chaos, she strode across the yard and met him face to face as he slowly picked himself up from the floor. 'No!' she said, standing hands on hips, eyeball to eyeball. 'No *way* am I going to let you get away with this!'

Seven

It was Wednesday and Day Two of Stevie's training programme. Helen got up early, determined not to let him beat her. If it took all day, every day of their half term holiday, she was going to tame that wild streak.

'Have you got your crash helmets and bullet-proof vests?' David Moore asked, as Helen checked the weather and got ready to go out to the barn. There was a fine drizzle and a grey sky; a typical start to a Lake District day.

'Ha-ha!' She wrinkled her nose at him.

'After yesterday I thought you might need them.'

Though he was joking, he wanted her to know that he was worried. 'You don't think you've bitten off more than you can chew, do you?'

Helen glanced at Hannah. Neither of them had slept much for thinking about Stevie. This morning Hannah was wearing a heavy bandage on her wrist where the donkey had wrenched himself free.

But Hannah wasn't ready to give in. 'No, we can do it,' she said firmly. She zipped up her jacket, ready to begin.

'Well, remember what your mum said about it,' he reminded them. 'If it comes to a choice between you and the donkey, we'd much rather have you two in one piece! In other words, if he's still playing up and throwing his weight around in a day or so's time, we'll have to think again about letting him stay here, OK?'

'Dad, that's not very long!' Helen protested. She knew they couldn't cure Stevie's bad temper overnight. It would take time and patience.

'Long enough for him to do a lot of damage.' He let them know that he wasn't joking and that his mind was made up.

'We'll try,' Hannah promised. 'And I'm sure

Stevie will be behaving better by the end of the week, honestly!'

Their dad softened. He nodded and smiled. 'I hope you're right. Go on, off you go. Knowing you two, you'll have him trained and ready to enter the Horse of the Year Show before we know it!' He winked and went on up to his dark-room.

Helen and Hannah went out into the damp farmyard. There was a smell of wet grass in the air, and a white mist hanging low over Doveton Fell. The bank holiday was over; everything in the valley was peaceful once more.

Hannah went first into the dark barn where Stevie had spent the night. The old door creaked open and let in a shaft of daylight; there he was, safely shut up in Solo's stall, watching suspiciously as they came in. But he didn't bray and kick up a fuss. Quietly, she took a fresh haynet from its hook and went to hang it up by his stall.

'Let him eat first,' she said, as Helen came up beside her. 'Then we can try getting the halter on him.' It was like starting all over again.

But they were patient. They went through it step by step, talking and coaxing the donkey to let them get near. 'At least he knows our voices now,' Helen said, eager to get him out into the yard. The halter was on, he was following the command to walk. 'Good boy!' she crooned at him, giving him a handful of ponynuts as a reward.

Out in the farmyard, Stevie took a good look round. There were the rabbits in their hutch, the hens pecking grain at the far side, Speckle and Socks keeping a safe distance in the kitchen doorway.

'Poor things,' Hannah sighed. Stevie was taking up all their time. 'We'll take you for a walk later, Speckle; when we've finished this training session.'

The dog wagged his tail and sat patiently waiting.

'Grooming time!' Helen said briskly. Stevie seemed quite calm and obedient. 'I know; I'll bring Solo in from the field and we can groom them both together!'

So she went and fetched the pony, who was glad to see her, and who would be a good example to Stevie. At the same time she decided to bring Sunny along, so he could join in the action. The piglet hated to be left out, and came scampering into the yard, snuffling for food. His little trotters clicked over the stone flags and he oinked with delight.

Stevie tossed his head impatiently. Who was this? Was it someone to pick a fight with? He eyed Solo, flicked his long ears, and decided not to argue with him. Then he looked with interest at the grooming brushes and combs which Helen brought out of the barn.

'Do you want to groom Stevie?' Hannah asked Helen, knowing very well what the answer would be.

Helen grinned. 'Thanks.' She took a stiff brush and began to work at the donkey's rough coat, talking as she brushed, moving evenly from his neck, down his shoulders and along his flanks. 'See, you like it! All you have to do is stand still like Solo. We'll soon have you both looking nice and smart!' She changed brushes and began on his mane. 'You've got hayseed in there!' she scolded. 'We have to get it out before it falls in your eyes.'

Soon both Solo and Stevie stood proudly in the middle of the farmyard, looking their best.

'Good boy, Solo!' Hannah patted his neck. 'This is your new friend, Stevie.'

Helen stood up straight and eased her back. 'Phew!' Grooming Stevie was hard work, but he'd been good as gold. It seemed that he was interested in the other animals and determined to show that anything they could do he could do too. Even when Sunny came fussing up, asking for his turn with the dandy brush, Stevie let him wriggle around his feet without even shifting.

It had been a good morning's work after the setback of the day before, and Hannah and Helen could relax. They decided to give Stevie a break from training and take Solo out on to the fell for the afternoon. So they rang Laura Saunders and arranged to meet up with her and her black thoroughbred, Sultan. Laura was a pony expert, and would be able to give them all sorts of tips on training Stevie too.

'When you're lifting his feet to clean his hooves, always stand at the side and face his rump,' she told them.

Hannah was riding Solo across the steep moor, with Helen cycling close behind on her mountain bike. 'What if he kicks?' she asked.

'Hang on to his foot and don't let him get away with it. He has to learn.' Laura had lived at Doveton

Manor all her life. She'd grown up with horses. The twins liked her, though she was a year or so older than them and was away at school during term time. 'And don't give up, even if he's stubborn,' she insisted. 'Donkeys are the same as ponies; once they trust you, they'll do anything for you!'

'Let's hope so.' Hannah told Laura that if they didn't manage to train Stevie, his chances of staying on at Home Farm were slim.

Laura listened quietly. As they turned the two ponies on to a bridle-path and began to walk them along the ridge, she gave a last piece of advice. 'From what you say, it won't be easy. There must be something wrong to make him go wild like that with other animals and with you. Normally a donkey wouldn't do that.' She thought it over. 'I think you should try and find out what it is.'

Helen rode hard to keep up. Her bike crunched over the rough track. 'Find out what's gone wrong with him in the past?' she queried.

Laura nodded. 'Yes. Then you stand a better chance of putting it right. It makes sense.'

They rode on, looking down the quiet hillside at the lake and village below.

'Easier said than done,' Helen sighed. They knew nothing about Stevie's past life; where he'd lived, who had owned him, or what had happened to make him the way he was.

And anyway, they were caught up hour by hour in getting to know their donkey and guess what he would do next. They learned what he liked and what he disliked, just how far they could push him to do as he was told, and when to give him a rest. By Wednesday evening, they had trained him to lift his feet when they gave the 'up!' command, and to come looking for a ponynut reward from their pockets when he'd done as he was told.

'Great stuff!' their dad told them. He'd come out to call them in for tea, and found them sitting on the farmyard gate, tired but pleased. Stevie was looking gentle as a lamb, safely tethered to the gate-post. 'Pity I've no ponynuts to give you two as a reward!'

They tutted and grinned.

'Will chicken and chips do instead?'

'Yum!' Hannah jumped down. 'I'm starving.'

'Me too.' Helen began to untie Stevie's rope.

'You mum will be home in ten minutes, and supper will be ready then,' he told them. 'Just time to get Stevie safely back into his stall and for you to wash your hands and get cleaned up.' He went off humming the old tune; 'All you need is love, *da-da da-da dum*!'

They felt great; another day, perhaps two with Stevie, and they would believe that they had won his trust. All his problems would be in the past, and he would settle down with Solo, Speckle, Sunny and the rest and become part of Home Farm. They were convinced that all you really did need was love.

'Come on, boy, walk!' Helen began to lead him across the yard. He walked smartly beside her, as Hannah held the barn door open.

All was well. Or was it? There was a warning sign; a tug on the halter, a sidestep, and then the throaty roar of a tractor coming up the lane from Fred Hunt's farm further down the hill.

Stevie heard it and went crazy again. He forgot where he was, forgot that Helen and Hannah were his friends, forgot everything except the roar of the engine and the tall tractor looming up the narrow lane. Its yellow roof showed above the wall tops, its great wheels rolled up the hill.

'Steady!' Helen tried to hang on. It was like yesterday; a dreadful action replay. Stevie kicked and lashed out. He didn't care who he hurt, what happened, as long as he broke free, away from the monster in the lane.

David Moore ran out of the house to see the donkey out of control, suddenly wild and terrifying, as his hooves hammered on to the yard and his back legs kicked out.

'It's cars!' Hannah gasped. She shielded her head with her arms and dodged to escape the flashing hooves. 'Don't you see? It's cars he's frightened of!' Every time Stevie had gone wild there had been a car involved.

Helen tried to grab hold of the loose halter, Stevie swerved away and the rope twisted out of her grasp. Fred Hunt's tractor stopped at the gate as the old farmer stared at the chaos in the yard.

Stevie bared his teeth and gave a terrified squeal.

'You're right!' Helen knew it was true; a car horn had frightened him at Lake View, and he'd been out of his mind with fear when he'd arrived at

Home Farm in the horse box. Then there was their mum's car yesterday teatime, and now this! 'Stevie hates cars!'

'Never mind that now!' Their father rushed to the gate and called for Fred Hunt's help. The two men stood firm and tried to corner Stevie. But he didn't know them. He didn't like their shouting voices or the huge tractor in the lane. He forgot everything the twins had taught him, reared up and hit out.

The twins watched helplessly, their good work ruined. Poor Stevie; why hadn't they seen it earlier?

It was their fault. They should have realised his nightmare dread before now. Cars sent him wild, like now, bucking and kicking like a crazy thing.

Mr Hunt and their father closed in on him. The donkey was cornered against the gate, with the tractor looming over him. His shrieks and brays echoed up and down the fell. Stevie was as wild and mean as ever.

Eight

'I'm glad he's not mine to look after!' Fred Hunt tilted his cap back from his forehead and tutted. There was much shaking of heads.

'What do you think, Fred?' David Moore asked. They'd managed at last to calm Stevie enough to lead him back to his stall. 'Is he a hopeless case?'

Hannah and Helen stood in the barn doorway, caught between looking after the donkey and listening to the discussion of his bad habits.

'Well, let's say he'll be a tough nut to crack.' The old farmer had dealt with plenty of stubborn animals in his time. He had a no-nonsense way of looking at things. 'And then, of course, there's always the fact that he might not be worth the effort you put into getting him right. He's only a donkey when all's said and done. It's not as if he's going to be worth much to you, not like the nice little pony you've got in the field back there.'

'*Only* a donkey!' Hannah bristled.

'He'd better not say anything against poor Stevie!' Helen clenched her fists. 'They wouldn't be talking this way if they realised what he must have been through.'

Behind them, Stevie kept up a stubborn clattering and banging.

'What's your advice, then?' Their dad looked worried. It had taken the two men all their strength to get the donkey back under control.

Fred Hunt wasn't unkind; he didn't want to hurt the twins' feelings. But he was practical. 'You say it's the sound of a car engine that sets him off, and you may well be right,' he admitted. 'But it begs the question of what you can do about it. The way I see it, he's always going to feel the same way about cars and you're never going to be able to take him anywhere near traffic. So unless you build him a stable way up on the fell, where cars can't get near him, you're stuck!' He shrugged and prepared to go on his way. The final words weren't what Helen and Hannah wanted to hear, he realised.

Helen kept up a brave face as Mr Hunt climbed into his tractor cab and trundled on up the hill. But inside she felt as if she'd had a hard kick in the stomach. The verdict on Stevie was bad, then. He was 'guilty' of hating cars. But she knew he didn't deserve to be punished for it.

'Dad?' Hannah went over and stood quietly beside him.

He thought in silence for a while.

'We don't want to send him back to Lake View, do we?'

'I don't know that we have much choice,' he answered sadly. 'But let's wait until this evening before we decide. We'll ask your mum what she thinks.' Head bowed, deep in thought, he wandered back into the house.

Feeling too hurt even to talk, Helen went to change Stevie's haynet and give him water after his ordeal with the tractor. Hannah followed her into the warmth and dark of the barn. She breathed in the scent of hay and straw, went up to a still frightened Stevie and patted his neck.

'Good boy, it's OK now!' She felt him quieten. Soon he stood still inside the stall, his head turned towards her, looking straight into her eyes. 'There, see; it's OK!'

'Is it?' Helen said quietly as she busily slung the haynet on to its hook.

'It has to be.' Hannah refused to think the worst. 'Listen, we think we know why Stevie goes wild, don't we? That's a step forward, not backwards.'

Helen backed off and disappeared into a dark corner to bring fresh straw for the floor of Stevie's stall. 'So what?' She didn't know who she was angry with, but she was so cross she almost cried. 'What good does that do?'

'It's like Laura said; once we know the reason, then we can start to put it right!'

Helen reappeared with an armful of straw. 'How?' she cried. She could hardly bear to look at Stevie now. 'What if Mum says he has to go?'

'That's her car coming up the lane.' Hannah felt Stevie flinch as he heard the distant noise. She fussed him and spoke gently to him. 'Helen, can you go and ask her not to drive right into the yard? It'll only upset Stevie all over again.'

So Helen ran into the lane to explain. Mary Moore parked the car on the grass verge and walked the last hundred metres home.

'Ah!' She listened carefully. 'Of course; cars spook him! That makes sense. Well done for spotting it.'

'It wasn't me, it was Hannah.'

'Well, good for Hannah. And you say your dad thinks we might have to send him back to Dotty?' Her mum put her bag down by the barn door and glanced in at Hannah and Stevie. Meanwhile, Speckle bounded out of the house to greet her. 'Hello, Speckle. Yes, it's me! Down!' she smiled and stroked the eager dog.

'I don't know. We're supposed to ask you.'

Mary Moore went in to see the donkey. 'How's our Problem with a capital "P"?'

The twins stood to one side as she reached out to stroke him. Stevie seemed to like the sound of her voice and her gentle touch. He settled and stood quiet.

'How do we solve your problem for you?' she

asked him. 'We can't ban all cars from Doveton, I'm afraid!'

Stevie shook his head and twitched his long ears.

'And we can't explain that the cars don't mean you any harm because you can't understand what we say.'

He snorted and stamped.

Hannah smiled. 'He says, "Yes, I can!".'

'So what can we do?' Mary was at a loss. She turned to see David Moore standing in the doorway.

'We don't even know if we're right about this car thing,' he pointed out. 'It's only a guess, isn't it?'

They had to admit he was right.

'As usual,' he joked. 'But do I take it that we're not ready to give up on Stevie just yet?'

Helen and Hannah turned to their mother, fingers crossed. Every ounce of their energy went into willing her to say no.

'No,' she said gently.

They breathed again. Stevie dipped his head and nuzzled up to her, as if he too understood.

'We can solve it, I know we can!' Hannah promised, though she had to admit that she still didn't know how.

* * *

'Look, if Stevie is scared of cars, there must be a reason!' Helen sat in bed that night, looking out of the window at the spreading branches of the horse-chestnut tree by the gate. There was silence in the farmyard, and out across the steep hillside to the high ridge of Doveton Fell.

'Maybe he had some kind of accident?' Hannah said sleepily. She lay tucked up under her duvet, tired out by the tussle to solve The Problem.

'That's it!' Helen was wide awake. 'An accident with a car. Stevie was hurt. Now he thinks all cars are dangerous.'

'And when he's stubborn and kicks out, it's not because he's angry, but because he's frightened.'

'Poor Stevie!' She remembered how Dotty must have forced him into the horse box to drive him to Home Farm. That had been terror in his eyes, not hate. 'Do you think anyone knows about him having an accident?'

'Not Miss Miller, or else she would have told us.'

'And she didn't mention it, did she? She says she doesn't know a thing about his life in Ireland.' Helen sighed and came to a full stop.

Then it was Hannah's turn to sit bolt upright. 'But I bet I know who *could* tell us!'

'Who?'

'Any vet who's treated him lately.'

'How?'

'Because there'd still be signs of an old injury, that's how!' She was excited. 'Don't you see? All we have to do is ring Mrs Freeman in the morning. She'll be able to tell us if we're right!'

Sally Freeman's voice showed no surprise when Hannah put the question over the phone. 'A car accident? An injury? Let me think.'

Helen and Hannah waited anxiously. Their whole training programme with Stevie depends on her answer.

'Come to think of it, I *was* surprised about one thing; an old break to his right foreleg. It was completely healed and not giving him any pain, but it had been a bad one. There's a rough ridge across the bone, and some scar tissue. I didn't pay it any attention at the time, but yes, of course, it could well have happened in an accident involving a car!'

Hannah thanked her and put down the phone.

'That's it!' Now they knew for sure why Stevie was badly behaved.

'What now?' Helen grabbed her jacket, ready to rush out to see him. So far this morning, all was quiet. Their mum had walked down the hill to her car, and set off freewheeling into the valley. Fred Hunt hadn't driven by in his tractor, and it was too early for any sightseers to have had breakfast and set off up the fell.

'Come on!' Hannah was out there first, with Speckle at her heel. 'We'll get Solo to help us, and all the other animals. They can make friends with Stevie and show him there's nothing to be afraid of round here!'

It was a plan that might work. They brought the pony in from the field into the yard. By the time Helen had fitted the halter on to Stevie and walked him out of the barn, the place was alive with hens pecking, Sunny the piglet busy-bodying, Socks the kitten pouncing at floating dandelion seeds, and Speckle barking a loud welcome.

The donkey halted mid-stride, ready to turn tail. Would he object to the crowded scene?

Helen clicked her tongue and gave him the

command to walk on. Across the yard, Hannah held out a handful of carrot slices to tempt him. Nervously Stevie moved forward with Helen at his side.

'Here, boy!' The juicy treat beckoned.

Then there was a flash of pink flesh, the quick patter of small trotters, a greedy oink as Sunny snaffled the carrots. Hannah's hand was empty.

'Oh!' Helen was afraid that Stevie might lose his temper. Any small thing could upset him.

Sunny shot off with a mouthful of carrots. He skipped between Speckle and Socks, then darted into the barn. Stevie pawed the stones with his front hoof. His head followed the path of the runaway piglet. Then he blinked and turned to Solo. No carrots, perhaps; but here was someone worth making friends with. He sidled across the yard to the grey pony with a look that said, 'I'm new here. How about showing me around?'

Solo tossed his mane; 'Do you fancy coming for a walk?'

'It's like they're talking to one another!' Hannah grinned with relief. 'And look, Speckle wants to come too.'

The dog bounded to the gate, waiting for the others to follow.

So Hannah took hold of Solo's bridle, while Helen led Stevie slowly out into the lane. They set off up the hill at a walking pace, letting the nervous newcomer get used to his surroundings.

'There's lots to look at,' Helen explained. She stopped and turned to show him the village nestling in the valley, the lake stretching into the distance, and the sheer fell sides beyond. As they walked on, Stevie turned his head with interest, this way and that. He learned to walk through the thick heather and across the steep slopes of grey shale. He felt the wind tug at his mane, watched as Hannah mounted Solo and begin to trek across the long ridge.

'You could learn to do that,' Helen told him as he looked hard at the rider and pony. 'No cars up here, see!'

He walked on willingly in the steps of Solo, with Speckle darting off through the heather and bobbing up far ahead or way below, then racing back to join them.

'You're brilliant!' Helen told him, at the end of the long morning's trek.

Stevie seemed to glow with pleasure. His eyes were bright, head up, ears pricked forward as they walked him back down to Home Farm.

'How did you get on?' David Moore asked them at lunch-time.

'OK.' Hannah didn't want to boast. She tucked in to a big plate of chips.

'No more outbreaks of teenage rebellion?'

'Who? Us or the donkey?'

'Ha!' He looked shrewdly at them. 'Not giving much away, are you?'

'No.' Helen munched on. It would be bad luck to speak too soon about the progress they had made.

'I saw you up on the fell this morning!' Laura Saunders called in that afternoon with a message for Mary Moore. 'I was out riding Sultan, but I didn't come across. I thought you might have your hands full with the donkey.'

Helen shrugged. 'It was his first time out on the fell.'

'Rather you than me,' Laura said. 'I hear he's been misbehaving again.' She kept her distance as Hannah trained Stevie to walk backwards on command.

'A bit.' There was no point telling her how much better Stevie was today, just in case . . . just in case he slipped back into his old ways! Helen didn't like to think about it, but she knew there was a long way to go before they could say that Stevie was cured.

'Stevie looks wonderful!' Mary Moore had glanced at the donkey as soon as she came home. She'd walked up the lane and seen him contentedly grazing in the field. 'He and Solo seem to be getting on like a house on fire!'

'We think we might be getting somewhere with him,' Hannah confessed shyly. 'Only we don't want to speak too soon.'

'Quite right.' Their mum sank into the armchair, kicked off her shoes and curled her feet under her. There was tea waiting, a tidy house, and windows open to the evening sun. 'I don't suppose you've taken him near any traffic yet?'

The twins shook their heads. 'We kept him away from the roads on purpose,' Hannah said.

'That'll be the real test, I suppose.' She sat back in the soft armchair and yawned. 'Still, it's a good start.'

Hannah and Helen nodded. That night, lying in bed, they made a big decision.

'Do you think we dare?' Hannah whispered across the small room. The ceiling sloped down towards the foot of her bed. Moonlight sent flickering shadows across its white surface. Helen had just suggested a thrilling idea.

'It's a bit of a risk, I know!'

'A *bit*!' Hannah echoed.

'OK, a *lot* of a risk. But wouldn't it be great if we could do it?' Helen was gripped by the new plan.

'We've only got three days.'

'Friday, Saturday, Sunday. But I think he'll be ready.'

'Open Day?' Hannah tried it out loud for herself. 'You want to take Stevie to Miss Miller's Open Day? But there'll be loads of cars there.'

'I know. But we won't take him if he doesn't want to go.' Helen had to admit that it was all up to Stevie in the end. 'We can try him out near some cars first; to teach him not to panic.'

'It won't be easy.' Hannah would hate to undo all the good work they'd done that day.

'But what do you think?'

She waited a while before she gave her answer. It would be an enormous challenge for the donkey. But yes, it would be a wonderful success. 'OK, we'll try!'

Sunday was Open Day at Lake View. They would take Stevie to meet up with the other donkeys again. He would be so well mannered and so perfectly trained that they would hardly recognise him.

'We'll do more than try!' Helen whispered. She put all her faith in him. 'If he can do this, there's nothing in this world that he won't be able to do!'

Nine

Stevie's grand entrance at Dotty Miller's Open Day was to be the best kept secret in Doveton.

'Don't tell anyone!' Helen made Hannah promise.

'Not even Mum and Dad?' Hannah asked.

She shook her head. 'It feels like bad luck if we mention it. And if we did tell someone, there'd be a lot of pressure on Stevie to behave properly.'

'Yes, that wouldn't help.' They had a long way to go before they could be sure that Stevie would be ready by Sunday. Today, Friday, they planned to walk him on the fell again. Then, when their mum came back from Nesfield, they would take him to have a good look at their car. That would be the hardest part so far, and a great test of how much Stevie had decided to trust them.

So for the third day they set about the business of working with Stevie. They fed him and groomed him, and taught him more commands without saying a word about their plan to anyone. From the moment they walked into the barn to greet him, through the long training session in the yard and the afternoon walk on the fell with Speckle and Solo, to the point when their mother's car headed up the lane in the early evening, the donkey was as good as gold.

The twins praised him and rewarded him. They said he was the cleverest donkey in the world; and the bravest and the most handsome. Stevie lapped it all up. He held his head high and obeyed their commands. He accepted Sunny's nosy, early morning grunts around his feet without stirring, and he stood patiently as Hannah picked stones from his hooves.

As for Solo, Stevie seemed to look up to him like an older brother, following in his footsteps when they walked across the mountainside, stopping when he stopped, copying his every movement.

'Now!' Hannah spoke softly to him as Helen tethered him to the gatepost and brushed him down. 'It's nearly time for Mum to come home from work. 'You'll hear the car coming up the hill, but she won't bring it too near, so you needn't be afraid.'

Stevie looked at her with his clever brown eyes, as if he understood every word.

'Yes, and when Mum's come to say hello, we're going to walk down the lane to look at the car,' Helen said firmly. 'You'll be safe with us, so there's no need to worry!'

Stevie snorted. He turned to look at Solo, who was tethered to the other gatepost.

'Solo can come too,' Helen promised. 'There's absolutely nothing to worry about!'

But it was with their hearts in their mouths that they set off to walk down the hill after their mum got back. In spite of what they'd told him, he'd heard the car and was already up to his old tricks. He pulled at the halter and rolled his eyes, all set to kick up a fuss if he didn't like what he saw.

'Come on, Solo, walk on!' Hannah went ahead

with the pony. The car was parked round a bend, still out of sight. Solo went confidently on.

Stevie hesitated.

'Walk – walk!' Helen urged. The hawthorn hedges on either side of the lane were covered in white blossom, the sun cast long shadows.

The donkey obeyed.

'Good boy!' They were on the curve of the bend, then round it, and the car was there on the grass verge, windscreen glinting in the sun.

Helen felt a quiver like an electric shock pass through the whole of Stevie's body. Hannah glanced round to see if they were following, her face anxious. 'Good boy, Stevie!' Helen whispered. 'Look at Solo; he doesn't mind! Come on, boy, walk!'

Gathering all of his courage, the donkey responded. He took a few short steps towards the car, came up alongside the pony. Solo waited, then when Stevie drew level, he deliberately stretched his neck over the car bonnet towards the hedge and took a nip at the juicy hawthorn leaves.

'See, nothing to it!' Helen hardly dared to breathe. There was too much power in the donkey for her to hold him back if he chose to lunge away.

But he knew what they were expecting of him, and he steeled himself to stand next to his metal enemy without flinching. This was just the kind of machine that had broken his leg and terrified him with its angry roar. But the twins were looking after him; he could trust them not to lead him into danger. So he stood firm in the narrow lane next to the car. For the first time in his life he overcame his fear.

'Is our car still in one piece?' David Moore met them coming back up the lane.

'Go and see!' Hannah beamed back at him. Stevie was in high spirits after his victory, and she had to hold him tight. There was a skip in his step as he led the way home ahead of Solo.

'No need. I can tell by your faces that it went off all right.'

'Brilliant!' Helen smiled. 'Stevie deserves a whole bag of ponynuts for what he just did!'

'Stop it, you're ruining his tough-guy image!' their dad warned. 'All this praise is bad for his street cred!'

They laughed. 'Deep down he's a softie,' Hannah insisted. She patted his soft white nose and led him on.

'You mean, your mum's got her soppy old donkey for when she retires, after all?' He stood to one side to let them past.

'Not so much of the soppy,' Helen warned. 'Stevie doesn't like being teased!'

And to show that he could take up his old image any time he felt like it, the donkey suddenly stopped. He planted his feet in the middle of the road, laid his ears flat and let out a loud, hoarse bray that split the air and echoed up and down the fell.

David Moore shot back against the wall. Solo snickered.

'That's right, you tell him, Stevie!' Helen laughed.

Hannah gave him his head and let him bray as long as he liked. 'No one's going to call *you* soppy and get away with it!' she grinned.

Ten

'Did you hear that donkey up at Home Farm making a racket last night?' Fred Hunt was having a grumble to Luke Martin in the village shop.

'I sure did. I guess you could've heard it over in Nesfield, 'Luke said with a grin. He spotted Hannah and Helen through the window, but didn't let on to the old farmer.

'Blooming nuisance,' he went on. 'Mind you, I did try to warn them. I told them they wouldn't be able to do much with a stubborn youngster like him.' He ignored the ring of the bell as the twins opened the door and sidled in.

'That's your expert opinion, is it, Fred?' Luke weighed out a bag of old-fashioned humbugs for him.

He sucked his teeth. 'Aye, well, once a donkey's got it into his head to dig in his heels and refuse to do as he's told, no amount of training will get him back on the right track.'

'Oh dear.' Luke rattled the sweets on to the scales. 'It looks like they didn't follow your advice, then. From what I hear, they're up on the fell with the young vandal morning, noon and night.' He winked at the twins.

'Barmy,' came the reply. 'Soft in the head when it comes to animals, those two.' The farmer took his sweets and delved in his pocket for his money.

Behind his back, Hannah stuck both hands on her hips, pretending to object. Helen covered her mouth to stop herself laughing.

'So you think they're wasting their time?' Luke persisted, one eye on the girls.

'I do. And meanwhile we have to put up with that terrible racket.' He took his change and turned towards them.

Helen and Hannah stared back, all innocence.

'Err-umph!' Mr Hunt coughed and swallowed. 'I was just saying, you're doing a grand job with that donkey!' he said, blushing bright red.

They smiled and thanked him, waited until he was out of the ship, then burst into giggles.

'I take it you don't agree with the expert?' Luke waited for them to pull themselves together.

'We're not saying a word!' Hannah told him. They'd come to the shop for a newspaper, just twenty-four hours before they put Stevie to the big test at Lake View.

'It'd be bad luck,' Helen explained. Even now they weren't certain that he would be ready. It was one thing for him to stand calmly beside their parked car; quite another to face a whole stream of traffic as it pulled through the gates at the donkey sanctuary. 'How many people have noticed the posters?' she asked, changing the subject.

'Loads,' Luke assured them. 'Lots of people have said how sweet the donkeys look, and Dotty was in here yesterday telling me that there's been a lot of interest already.'

'That's great.' Hannah paid for the newspaper,

anxious to cycle back home and begin work with Stevie.

'Are you sure you don't want to tell me how you're getting on with your rebel donkey?' Luke was curious. 'It looks to me like you've got something up your sleeves!'

The twins smiled identical, secretive smiles.

'Come to Dotty's Open Day tomorrow!' Helen told him. 'We're not saying anything until then!'

Meanwhile there was work to do.

'Stand!' Helen told Stevie. She was armed with brushes and cloths, scissors and combs. The donkey looked on with a worried expression. What were all these things for?

'We're going to give you a special beauty treatment,' Hannah told him. 'Tomorrow is your big day, and you have to look your best.'

The other animals spied the water in the bucket and made a quick exit. Sunny trotted off to the field to join the goats and Solo, while Socks found a warm windowsill and Speckle crept off into the kitchen. Soon there was only Stevie standing there, ready for the treatment.

'First the wash and blow-dry!' Helen announced. She plunged a cloth into the warm water, wrung it out and firmly rubbed at the stains on Stevie's dark-brown coat. Then she dipped his tail into the soapy bucket and dried it with a towel. After this it was brushing and more brushing until their arms ached. But in the end his coat was shiny as a nut. 'Now for the short back and sides!' Helen said.

'Not too much,' Hannah promised, going to work on his straggly tail with a pair of scissors. Stevie turned his head to watch. 'Don't worry, I'm only cutting a tiny bit!' she laughed.

Next his spiky mane had to be combed and trimmed. 'Tricky!' Helen said as she watched Hannah snip at the upright ends.

'What do you think?' Hannah stood back at last. Stevie's black mane stood up in an even ridge along his neck.

'Pretty good.' Helen admired the smart effect. 'Feet!' she ordered, lifting the bewildered donkey's hooves one by one, picking them out with a hoof-pick and finally polishing them with hoof-oil.

'Beautiful!' They stood back at last from the all-over beauty treatment. He gleamed from head to foot, and with his smart new haircut they hardly recognised the sulky, stubborn donkey they'd first met.

Stevie didn't look quite so sure. In fact, he showed a definite desire to roll on the floor.

'No!' Hannah cried, dashing forward to take hold of his halter. 'You'll undo all our good work!'

'Whew-whew!' A whistle drifted down from the attic window; Mr Moore's favourite lookout. 'Who's a pretty boy, then?'

The twins frowned back. 'You're embarrassing him!' Hannah protested.

'Is this the same donkey?'

'Da-ad!' Helen took the bucket and emptied it down the drain. Then she cleared away the brushes. 'Take no notice,' she told Stevie. 'He's only jealous!'

'Now, the big question is, how are you going to get all the way to Lake View?' Mary Moore asked. It was early on Sunday morning; a clear, cool day, with sun forecast.

Hannah explained the plan. 'We'll take Solo and Stevie . . .'

Speckle came up and poked his nose against her lap.

'Oh yes, and Speckle can come too! Helen and I will take turns riding Solo. The other one will walk with Stevie, down into Doveton, then up out of the valley to the donkey sanctuary. We aim to get there just before ten o'clock.'

Their mum stopped brushing her hair and looked at her watch. 'How long will it take?'

'About an hour.'

'And is Dotty expecting you?'

Helen shook her head. 'It's a surprise.'

'Well, if anything goes wrong, your father will be at home, won't you, David?'

'Uh.' Their dad came downstairs in his pyjamas.

'That means "yes"!' She smiled and gave them a hug. 'Good luck!'

'Thanks,' they murmured.

'And tell Stevie that I know he can do it!' Last night she'd been able to drive the car right into the yard without him being spooked. 'Every day he takes a giant step forward!'

'And this is the really big one,' Helen said, her eyes bright with excitement as they went to get ready.

* * *

By eight-thirty they'd done all their chores and brought Solo in from the field. Helen had polished his tack and saddled him. He stood impatient to be off on a fine morning's ride. Now it was time to bring Stevie out of his stall. Hannah went in to fetch him, so nervous that she could hardly unbolt the door. But the moment she saw him, she smiled.

'Come and look at this!' she called to Helen. During the night Stevie had managed to mess up his smooth hairdo and gleaming coat by sticking his whole head into the haynet. Now he was covered in seeds, with strands of hay poking out of his thick mane and fringe.

So they had to get a move on. Out with the brushes and combs; lots of elbow-grease and no time to be nervous. Stevie stood enjoying the attention, nuzzling up to Solo for a quiet chat.

'Nine o'clock,' Hannah gasped. They'd finished just in time. Now it was on with the halter, a quick goodbye to their dad, and time to leave.

'Good luck!' he called after them. No jokes, no teasing from him on this special morning.

They set off briskly; Hannah riding Solo and Helen leading Stevie, with Speckle walking behind. The lane was quiet, except for a hedgehog that scuttled across the road and Fred Hunt's cat sitting watching them from the wall top.

'Good heavens above!' A man's voice came from beyond the wall. Fred was in the field with his cattle; Hannah saw his cap and old tweed jacket. Now he was coming to the gate and leaning over it. 'That's not the same donkey, is it?'

'It is, it's Stevie!' Helen held him steady and whispered for him to stand still. Stevie obeyed like an angel.

'Well, I'll be blowed!' The old man was lost for words. He stood and stared at the willing donkey.

'Walk on, Stevie. Good boy!' She led him on, head high, enjoying every moment, as Mr Hunt stood gazing after them.

'Your turn to ride Solo,' Hannah told her as they came on to the village road and stopped outside the gates of Doveton Manor. She dismounted, ready to take Stevie's lead rope.

'Wow!' Laura Saunders came running down the drive. 'He looks absolutely fantastic!' She stopped at the gate, hardly able to believe her eyes. 'You two did a great job!' she gasped.

Stevie knew he was being admired. He whisked his tail and stamped his foot.

'Show-off!' Hannah told him, but she knew he deserved every bit of Laura's praise.

'Where are you going? Not to Lake View by any chance?' The older girl sounded envious.

'How did you guess?' Helen smiled as she mounted Solo. 'Do you and Sultan want to come too?' Laura was dressed for riding in her jodhpurs and hard hat.

'Sure?'

The more the merrier, they said. So the procession down the village street grew longer. Now Speckle led the way past Luke's shop, then Solo and Helen, Hannah leading Stevie, and last of all came Laura on Sultan.

'Very smart!' Luke called from the shop doorway. He gave them a wink and a wave as they walked on.

In the distance, a car crossed over the T-junction leading to Nesfield, its engine a tiny whir on the breeze.

Stevie heard it and flattened his ears. But Hannah whispered to him to walk on and he hardly hesitated.

'Fingers crossed,' Helen said from up ahead. Soon they would be on that road and Stevie would have to cope with cars, motor-bikes, lorries; who knew what?

More cars whizzed along the main road. Now they were in sight; little shiny insects buzzing up the hill. The donkey went doggedly on, following in Solo's footsteps, trusting the twins not to lead him into danger.

And then they were at the junction and on the road itself. Lake View was a white speck on the hillside. A small motor-bike came up from behind and overtook their procession. Stevie bridled and sidestepped, but Hannah held firm and told him to walk on. 'Be brave,' she murmured. 'We won't let anything hurt you.'

'Car!' Laura signalled from the back of the group. She was wearing a clear 'Slow Down for Horses' sign on her back. The driver read it and steered well clear.

This time Stevie's jitters were worse. He pulled at the halter and made as if to buck.

But once more Hannah held fast. 'No!' she said firmly. To her relief, Stevie settled and kept on walking. 'Good boy!'

Helen turned in her saddle. 'So far so good!'

'You can do it,' Hannah urged. She felt Stevie stare straight ahead, determination in every step.

It seemed the worst was over. Cars swept by as they made their way up the hill, and each time Stevie was calmer, more sure of himself.

'It already looks pretty busy up there,' Laura called, pointing out the cars parked in the drive-way at Lake View. 'That's good for Miss Miller, but I hope it's not too much for Stevie!'

They fell silent as they covered the last stretch of road. It was true; the Open Day was already a great success. They could see a small crowd gathered by the fence, looking into the field where the donkeys were kept. Children climbed up for a better look, while grown-ups stood back and talked. Outside the front door of the house was Dotty Miller serving coffee, orange juice and biscuits.

'Here goes!' Helen turned Solo into the drive.

'Walk on, Stevie!' Hannah gave him no chance to refuse.

Bringing up the rear, Speckle, Laura and Sultan urged him forward, between the rows of parked cars.

'By Jove!' Dotty Miller's voice rang out. She left the juice and custard creams and strode to meet them. 'This is absolutely amazing! However did you do it?'

Helen dismounted grinning all over her face. 'It was hard work,' she admitted.

'I'll bet it was.' The tough old lady was full of admiration. By now several of the visitors had come to see what was going on. A little dark-haired boy came up to Stevie and stroked his cheek.

'But he looks an absolute treat. I can't get over the difference!' Miss Miller said. She led them slowly up the hill towards the house.

This was it; the moment they had dreamed about. Stevie walked proudly on, soaking up the attention, strutting in front of the crowd.

But there was a disturbance down at the gate. A large vehicle was squeezing into the drive, rattling and rocking as it came. Helen and Hannah glanced back, saw a huge old horse box being towed by a Land Rover coming up between the rows of cars.

'I say!' Dotty objected. 'Can't he see there isn't room?'

But the driver seemed dead set on squeezing by.

'Oh no!' Laura slipped from the saddle, her face anxious. Even Sultan disliked the loud racket.

Hannah held on to Stevie. 'Stand!' The old nightmare was beginning again; a horse box looming, a roar of an engine, a cloud of diesel fumes. The donkey tossed his head and bared his teeth. She felt the fear shoot through him, trembling along every nerve. 'Stand still, Stevie!' she urged.

In a split second Helen made a decision. She slipped Solo's reins into Hannah's free hand and ran down the hill. The Land Rover was only twenty metres from Stevie, and still roaring on. She stood in its path, arms wide, waving furiously at the driver. 'Stop!' she yelled.

He drew up with a screech of brakes. Clouds of black smoke pumped out of his exhaust, the horse box rocked and came to a rattling halt.

Hannah watched and prayed. 'Good boy, Stevie,' she breathed. 'Look at Solo; he's not a bit worried!'

The pony nuzzled up to him with a word of friendly advice.

Stevie looked and listened. The crowd stood back, wondering what would happen. It was obvious that the donkey was frightened, and in this small space, would he panic and let fly with his hooves? Dotty Miller stood between them and Stevie, keeping guard.

Helen went to speak to the driver; a youngish man in a white T-shirt, with short fair hair. She explained the situation and the man agreed to back down the drive.

'I'm not very good at towing this great big thing,' he confessed. 'I'm sorry if I've scared your ponies.'

'See!' Hannah whispered in Stevie's ear as the horse box slid back down the drive. 'We told you we wouldn't let anything hurt you!'

He gave a deep sigh. Gradually the trembling stopped and he relaxed. His head went up and he put on a show; 'What's all the fuss?' He tossed his smart mane and shook his head. 'Only a little horse box, nothing to be worried about!'

'Remarkable!' Miss Miller dropped her guard. The crowd began to split up and go off to look at the other donkeys. The crisis was over.

'Let's go!' Stevie seemed to say to Solo and

Sultan. He had his tough-guy image to think of, after all.

Helen ran back to join Hannah and take Solo's rein. The little boy who had made friends with Stevie stood nearby.

'He's lovely!' he told his father, clinging on to his hand and beginning to plead. 'I like him best. Can we take him home with us?'

Hannah grinned at Helen, then led Stevie across to explain. 'This donkey doesn't need a new home. He's already got one!'

The boy's face fell, but only for a moment. 'He's my favourite donkey. Where does he live?'

'With us,' Helen told him. Her smile seemed to spread through her whole body as she linked arms with Hannah.

'At Home Farm!' they said, full to the brim with pride.

HOME FARM TWINS
Jenny Oldfield

66127 5	Speckle The Stray	£3.50	❏
66128 3	Sinbad The Runaway	£3.50	❏
66129 1	Solo The Homeless	£3.50	❏
66130 5	Susie The Orphan	£3.50	❏
66131 3	Spike The Tramp	£3.50	❏
66132 1	Snip and Snap The Truants	£3.50	❏
68990 0	Sunny The Hero	£3.50	❏
68991 9	Socks The Survivor	£3.50	❏

All Hodder Children's books are available at your local bookshop or newsagent, or can be ordered direct from the publisher. Just tick the titles you want and fill in the form below. Prices and availability subject to change without notice.

Hodder Children's Books, Cash Sales Department, Bookpoint, 39 Milton Park, Abingdon, OXON, OX14 4TD, UK. If you have a credit card you may order by telephone – (01235) 831700.

Please enclose a cheque or postal order made payable to Bookpoint Ltd to the value of the cover price and allow the following for postage and packing:
UK & BFPO – £1.00 for the first book, 50p for the second book, and 30p for each additional book ordered up to a maximum charge of £3.00.
OVERSEAS & EIRE – £2.00 for the first book, £1.00 for the second book, and 50p for each additional book.

Name ....

Address ....

....

....

If you would prefer to pay by credit card, please complete:
Please debit my Visa/Access/Diner's Card/American Express (delete as applicable) card no:

Signature ....

Expiry Date ....